Finn's Causeway Adventure belongs to:

_____

_____

For Charlie and Kristie with love
- Lauren

For Mum and Dad
- Dave

Text copyright © 2006 Lauren Graham
Illustrations copyright © 2006 Dave Orchard

Published in Ireland by O'Donnell Press,
12 Coolemoyne Park, Jordanstown, Co. Antrim BT37 0RP
Telephone: 028 9096 6493
Email address: b.odonnell93@ntlworld.com
www.odonnellpress.com

A CIP catalogue record of this book is available from the British Library.

Printed in Ireland by GPS Colour Graphics Ltd.
Repro Scanning by iris colour.

ISBN 0-9553325-1-6

1 2 3 4 5 6 7 8 9 10

O|O O'DONNELL PRESS

Finn's
Causeway Adventure

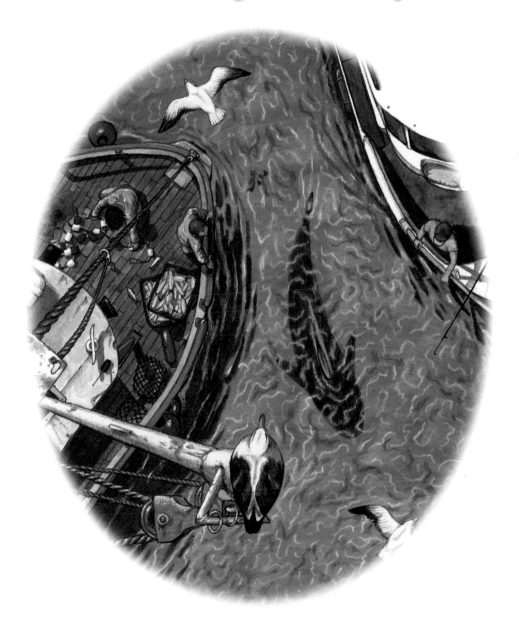

By Lauren Graham

Illustrated by Dave Orchard

The summer sun had again begun to warm the ocean waters. It was time for Finn to set off for his holiday home on the North Coast of Ireland. He swam excitedly through the deep, dark waters as quickly as he could and soon he spotted familiar coastline ahead. It was the Causeway Coast.

Finn was usually a shy shark. He had been coming to the Causeway Coast every summer since he was a baby. To him, this was the most beautiful place in the whole world. Usually he stayed well out at sea, away from the shore, meeting only the occasional passing boat, but this year he was feeling a little more confident and was looking for adventure. He was determined that he was going in for a close-up look at this dramatic coastline.

As he swam towards the shore, he saw strange shapes that rose out of the sea and onto the land. Finn swam nearer to take a closer look. Rocks in the shape of hexagons were joined together to form an unusual pathway that led from the seabed to the cliffs above. Children were climbing over this causeway and playing in rock pools close to the water's edge while their parents sat relaxing on the rocks, sunbathing in the splendid summer sunshine.

Finn swam right up to the water's edge and raised his head.
As he stared upwards, he caught sight of a little boy's face
looking down into the water towards him. For a moment their
eyes met and Finn's mouth opened into a wide smile that
showed his sparkling white teeth.

Suddenly, the young boy leapt to his feet, as if terrified, yelling, 'Fin, fin!' Screams filled the air as people ran inland, away from the rocks and away from Finn. Poor Finn was so shocked that he swam through the sea as quickly as he could. He was quite confused. Lots of questions raced around his head. Had he met this boy before? How did the boy know his name? Why had the boy been so frightened and why was everyone screaming?

Finn swam swiftly, following the coast until at last he reached a little island. A rope bridge led from the island to rugged cliffs along the shore. The bridge swayed slightly in the breeze as people slowly moved across it. Finn swam through the waters below, enjoying the spectacular sight above.

Suddenly he saw the people on the bridge pointing down towards him. They began to yell, 'Fin, fin!'

Finn couldn't believe it. He had been recognised again. How could these people possibly know him? Confused and a little frightened, Finn swam out to the safety and security of the deep ocean.

The next day, Finn decided once again to return to the shore. This time, he thought it wise to avoid the causeway and the rope bridge. He instead swam towards a beautiful beach. Deep, golden sand stretched from the water's edge to the white rocks. The beach was crowded. Barbecues were sizzling and families were eating delicious picnics. Children were playing ball games and building gigantic sandcastles surrounded by moats.

As Finn came closer to the beach, he couldn't help but notice the wind surfers and body boarders. They rode on huge waves that formed deep out at sea and swept swiftly inland to crash in a layer of white foam at the water's edge. 'What fun', thought Finn, 'I too must have a go'. He caught the crest of a wave and let it pull him towards the shore. The wave raised him higher and higher, faster and faster, until **SMASH**, he collided with a wind surfer and sent the poor lad hurtling through the air until he landed with a splash in the water some distance away.

Other wind surfers spotted what had happened and began to yell, 'Fin, fin!' as they ran screaming from the water. Everyone fled from the sea and crowds ran down the beach, towards the water's edge. Gathered on the wet sand they stood watching and yelling as poor Finn tried in vain to swim away. This poor shark's stomach was stuck in the sand at the bottom of the sea.

News of Finn's misfortune soon
began to spread and the crowds
on the beach got bigger and
bigger. By late afternoon, the
coastguard and the Portrush
lifeboat had arrived to rescue Finn
from his sandy fate. Carefully
they placed ropes around his body
and tugged him off the sandy
seabed. As he floated out to sea,
the crowd on the shore clapped
and cheered.

Once they had reached the deep water, Finn's rescuers loosened the ropes and Finn was free once more. He manoeuvred magnificently deeper into the Atlantic Ocean, until he was finally out of sight.

Shocked and frightened by his ordeal, it took some weeks
before Finn once again swam close enough to see the
Causeway Coast. He still loved his holiday home but he had
found enough adventure. He was happy to become a shy shark
once more.

For the rest of the summer only the crew of an occasional
boat spotted Finn. He stayed well out at sea and admired his
beautiful Causeway Coast from afar.

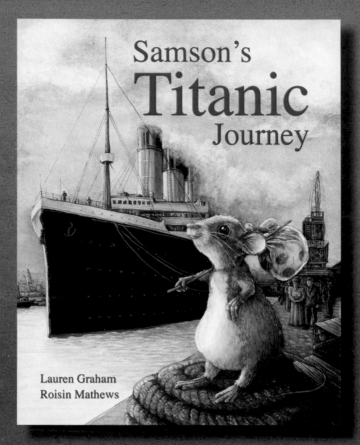

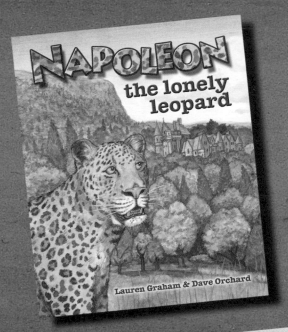

Napoleon the lean leopard spent his days running with his friends through the beautiful plains of Africa. Life was wonderful, wild and free. But one day, Napoleon was attacked. He was so badly injured that he was forced to leave his home and friends to begin a new life in a zoo far away.

Would Napoleon ever find a new friend or would he be a lonely leopard for evermore?.........

ISBN 0-9546163-7-5 £5.99

What will Pete find at the end of his rainbow?

Pete seems like a typical little boy, but something is not quite right. Pete wishes it would rain. He won't go out in the sunshine and Mum and Granny can't understand why, especially when he rushes out after a heavy shower. But it's not the rain that Pete is interested in, it's what sometimes comes after.

Follow Pete as he chases a rainbow trying to reach the end. What is he hoping to find and will he get there in time?

ISBN 0-9546163-1-6 £4.99

Ollie the ostrich loved to race. One day he ran so fast that he left his family far behind. While on his own he met Weaver Bird, Lion, Giraffe and Elephant. But it was only when Ollie met Cheetah that he was glad he could **run like the wind.**

ISBN 0-9546163-6-7 £5.99

www.odonnellpress.com